A NOTE TO PARENTS

Reading Aloud with Your Child

Research shows that reading books aloud is the single most valuable support parents can provide in helping children learn to read.

- Be a ham! The more enthusiasm you display, the more your child will enjoy the book.
- Run your finger underneath the words as you read to signal that the print carries the story.
- Leave time for examining the illustrations more closely; encourage your child to find things in the pictures.
- Invite your youngster to join in whenever there's a repeated phrase in the text.
- Link up events in the book with similar events in your child's life.
- If your child asks a question, stop and answer it. The book can be a means to learning more about your child's thoughts.

Listening to Your Child Read Aloud

The support of your attention and praise is absolutely crucial to your child's continuing efforts to learn to read.

- If your child is learning to read and asks for a word, give it immediately so that the meaning of the story is not interrupted. DO NOT ask your child to sound out the word.
- On the other hand, if your child initiates the act of sounding out, don't intervene.
- If your child is reading along and makes what is called a miscue, listen for the sense of the miscue. If the word "road" is substituted for the word "street," for instance, no meaning is lost. Don't stop the reading for a correction.
- If the miscue makes no sense (for example, "horse" for "house"), ask your child to reread the sentence because you're not sure you understand what's just been read.
- Above all else, enjoy your child's growing command of print and make sure you give lots of praise. *You are your child's first teacher — and the most important one. Praise from you is critical for further risk-taking and learning.*

—Priscilla Lynch
Ph.D., New York University
Educational Consultant

This is for Bernette, Grace,
Gina, and Edie, who bring
out the best in us.
—E. R. & D. B.

The artist and the editors would like
to thank Elaine Raphael for her creative help
in the painting of the illustrations.

Text copyright © 1998 by Margo Lundell.
Illustrations copyright © 1998 by Don Bolognese.
All rights reserved. Published by Scholastic Inc.
HELLO READER!, CARTWHEEL BOOKS, and the CARTWHEEL BOOKS logo
are registered trademarks of Scholastic Inc.

Library of Congress Cataloging-in-Publication Data

Lundell, Margo.
    Lad, a dog: the bad puppy / retold by Margo Lundell;
based on the book by Albert Payson Terhune; illustrated by Don Bolognese.
        p.   cm.—(Hello reader! Level 4)
    "Cartwheel books."
    Summary: While his mate Lady is ill in the hospital, Lad looks after their
puppy Wolf, who gets into a lot of mischievous trouble and even endangers
both their lives.
    ISBN 0-590-92981-X
    1. Dogs—Juvenile fiction. [1. Dogs—Fiction. 2. Animals-Infancy—
Fiction.] I. Terhune, Albert Payson, 1872–1942. Lad, a dog. II. Bolognese,
Don, ill. III. Title. IV. Series.
PZ10.3.L967Lae   1997
[Fic]—DC20   96-27681
                                                            CIP
                                                            AC

10 9 8 7 6 5 4 3 2 1   8 9/9 0/0 01 02

                    Printed in the U.S.A.   24

                First printing, February 1998

LAD, A DOG

The Bad Puppy

Retold by Margo Lundell

Based on the book by Albert Payson Terhune

Illustrated by Don Bolognese

Hello Reader! — Level 4

SCHOLASTIC INC. Cartwheel B·O·O·K·S ®

New York   Toronto   London   Auckland   Sydney

L ad was in love.
A young female collie had come
to live at the Place.

Her name was Lady.
Lad thought Lady was perfect
in every way.
Before long, Lady was as important to Lad
as the sun coming up in the morning.
Lad was a powerful, purebred collie.
But he was a gentle giant.
The heart in Lad's mighty chest
was huge.
He gave it gladly to Lady.

The Place was a large estate
in New Jersey.
It was wonderful for the two dogs.
There were thick woods
to roam in side by side.
There were squirrels to chase
and rabbits to trail.
In the summer heat, the two dogs
cooled off in the lake together.

Life was wonderful in winter, too.
There were long walks in the snow.
There was a big, warm house.
On cold nights the two collies lay
in front of the living room fire.
The master and mistress sat nearby.
Lad was happy when he was close to them.
He loved Lady.
But he worshipped the master
and mistress.

One year everything changed.
Lady had puppies early in the fall.
There were three collie pups,
but two of them soon died.
No one knew why.
The puppy that lived
was a wild little ball of fluff.
The mistress named him Wolf.

After Lady became a mother,
Lad was lonely.
Lady would not run in the woods
with him anymore.
She spent all her time with Wolf.
Lad could not understand it.
Why did Lady care so much
about the puppy?

One day in November, Lady looked sick.
Her nose was hot and dry.
The master asked the vet
to come to the house.
"It looks like distemper," the vet said.
"Of course, that's very bad."
The vet put Lady in his car.

They were going to the animal hospital.
Lad growled quietly.
He didn't want Lady to go.
The master held him back.
"It's all right, Laddie," the master said.
"It's the only way to save her."

Then Lady was gone.
Lad walked into the house
and crawled under the piano.
He did not come out
for the rest of the day.
The big collie was very unhappy.

The next morning Lad looked
everywhere for Lady.
He hoped she had come back
during the night.
But she hadn't.

Wolf found Lad that morning.
The puppy wanted to play.
He ran up to Lad and bit his ear.
He chewed the big dog's nose.
He tried to bite Lad's neck.
Finally Wolf grew sleepy
and curled up next to Lad.
Lad stared down at Wolf.
He remembered how much
Lady loved the puppy.
She was gone — maybe forever.
Wolf was alone and needed help.
Lad began to lick Wolf's furry head.
Lad was going to take care of
Lady's puppy.

Keeping up with Wolf was not easy.
The puppy was everywhere.
He chased the mistress' chickens.
He barked at every bird.
He grew bigger and stronger every day.

Lad tried to teach Wolf how to behave.
He taught the puppy not to eat
everything he found.
One day Wolf began chewing
the mistress' hat.
Lad picked up the puppy.
He wouldn't put Wolf down
until the puppy dropped the hat.

Lad was firm with Wolf,
but he was good to the puppy, too.
Lad ran with Wolf in the woods.
He led Wolf to the lake
and taught him to swim.

Weeks went by.
Lad was busy with Wolf,
but he did not forget Lady.
One day the vet stopped by
to talk to the master about her.
Lad knew that this was the man
who had taken Lady away.

Lad was the best dog in the world.
But that day he forgot everything
the master had taught him.
He ran across the room
and attacked the vet.
The vet threw up his arms.
"Lad!" the master shouted.
It was a sharp command.
Lad dropped to the floor.
"Lad!" the master repeated.
The great collie began to shake.
Lad knew he had broken the law.

The master ordered Lad out of the house.
"Don't beat him," the vet said.
"He knows I took Lady away."
"He's lucky you understand,"
the master answered.
"I won't beat him.
But send me a bill for that torn coat."

When December came,
Lady was still gone.
The days were cold and snowy.
Wolf loved the snow.
He rolled in it.
He bit it.
He barked at it.

December was so cold the lake froze.
The ice was strong.
Wolf was surprised.
He remembered swimming with Lad.
He could not understand
what had happened to the water.
But what fun to walk on it!
The puppy had never been happier.
He spent hours at the lake,
running and slipping on the ice.

Drip. Drip. Drip.
In January there was an early thaw.
It was warm for three days.
Snow melted.
The ice on the lake grew slushy.

On the third day Lad and Wolf
ran down to the lake together.
The top of the lake looked wet.
Wolf didn't mind.
He raced onto the watery ice.

When Lad reached the lake,
he stopped at the edge.
He sniffed the air.
Grrrrr.
Lad growled a warning to Wolf.
Wolf turned and looked back.
Then the eager puppy
ran further out onto the ice.

CRAAACK.
Wolf had jumped onto a thin patch of ice.
It could not hold him.
The ice around the puppy
broke into chunks.
He floated for a moment on a cake of ice.
Then he slid into the cold, dark water.

Wolf splashed in the freezing water.
Then he tried to climb onto the
ice again.
He slipped and slid.
He fell back into the water.
The scared puppy began to bark.
He barked and splashed
and howled for help.

The master and mistress were
coming up the driveway in the car.
They heard Wolf's cries.
"He's in trouble!" the master said.
They climbed out of the car
and ran toward the lake.
It was a long way to run.
They couldn't reach the lake in time
to save Wolf.

But Lad was already there.
When Wolf began to howl,
Lad had rushed onto the ice.
He trotted close to the hole
where Wolf was swimming.

Suddenly Lad could feel the ice
breaking under his weight.
Then he sank into the lake, too.
Brrrrrr.
The cold water took Lad's breath away.
He began swimming
toward the frozen puppy.

Lad reached Wolf and picked him up
by the back of the neck.
He swam with the puppy to the edge
of the hole.
Then Lad used all his strength
and rose half out of the water.
He threw Wolf up onto solid ice.

Wolf's sharp claws dug into the ice.
He found his footing
and scrambled ashore.

Wolf was out of danger,
but *Lad* was in trouble.
The big collie had saved Wolf,
but the effort was too much.
Lad fell back into the lake and sank
under the water.

The current caught Lad and
pulled him sideways.
When Lad tried to come up again,
the top of his head hit something.
It was ice.
Lad was trapped under the ice with no air
to breathe.

Lad held his breath and swam.
Finally he found the hole in the ice.
His head burst out of the water.
He sputtered and panted.
He could breathe again.
By then the master had reached the lake.
He stretched out on the ice
and crawled toward Lad.
"Here, Laddie! Come on, boy!"
Lad heard the master calling.
Lad tried to drag himself
up onto the ice.

Twice Lad almost pulled himself
out of the water.
Each time the ice broke underneath him.
Then the tired dog tried once more.
This time the master was close by.
He reached out and grabbed
Lad's wet ruff.

"You can do it, Laddie!" he urged.
The master pulled, and Lad struggled.
"Come on, Lad!"
Finally the collie was out of the water
and up on top of the ice.

Lad and the master crawled
carefully back to shore.
Then the master sat on the ground
and hugged the wet dog.
"You're all right, Lad!" he whispered.

Lad shook himself off.
Then he turned toward the mistress.
He wanted her to hug him, too.
He wanted her kind words.
But the mistress was not alone.
"Laddie, look who's back," she said.

Poor tired Lad was in a daze.
He stared at the dog in his path.
Could it be?
Yes, it was *Lady.*
"She's well again, Laddie," the mistress said.
"We drove over this morning
and picked her up."
But Lad did not hear all the words.
Lady was biting his ear.
She wanted him to run and play.
Lad's world was right once more.
Wolf was safe,
and Lady was
home at last.

— ❖ —

— *About Lad* —

The famous collie lived with the
talented animal and nature writer,
Albert Payson Terhune, and his wife,
in Pompton Lakes, New Jersey. The
"Place" was a wooded estate called
Sunnybank.

A series of magazine stories about Lad
were published during World War I.
The stories were very popular. After the
war, the stories were published in a book.
The book about Lad sold very well.
The brave, loyal dog became so popular
that people would drive to Sunnybank
uninvited "to see where Lad lived."
The author was finally forced to put
up gates and keep them closed.

Terhune went on to write stories about
other dogs, but he was always best
known for the tales he told about the
collie. There was no other dog like Lad.
The author said it well in his dedication
to the book:

This book is dedicated

to the memory of

LAD

thoroughbred in body and soul